Reading Together

The Old Woman and the Red Pumpkin

Read it together

The Old Woman and the Red Pumpkin is a new telling of a traditional Indian folktale about a brave grandmother who outwits the wild animals in the forest on her journey home.

Hearing you read this story aloud and looking at the beautiful illustrations will take your child on a journey to a different time and place.

She left her house, walked through the markets, past the river and into the deep, dark forest.

"Ach-cha," said the tiger. "Go and get fat, and ..."

"when you come back, I'll eat you."

There are lots of patterns in this book to help your child remember the story and join in. There's the strong pattern of three animals met along the way, and lots of repetition. All help with predicting what happens next.

Once they know a book well, children can have a go at reading to you. At first they may "read" by remembering the story and retelling it in their own words.

Once upon a time there was an old woman who was so crooked that she needed a stick to hold her up.

When your child is struggling over a word you can help them make a good guess by pointing to a picture which gives a clue, or reading to the end of the sentence and asking what would make sense. Praise good guesses even if they don't match the word in the book. Readers need the confidence to take risks!

You can encourage your child to look more closely at words and letters by pointing out similarities between words on the page. Ask if they can find some.

This is a story in the true folktale tradition, where good triumphs over evil. You can talk to your child about this story and others with similar endings.

We hope you enjoy reading this book together.

For Joyce Biswas and Helen and Herbert Gordon
B.B.

For Nanna Leather
R.M.

First published 1998 by Walker Books Ltd
87 Vauxhall Walk, London SE11 5HJ

2 4 6 8 10 9 7 5 3 1

Printed in Great Britain

ISBN 0-7445-4888-8

A Bengali folk tale
translated and adapted by

Betsy Bang

Illustrated by

Rachel Merriman

There was once an old woman who was so bent over she had to hold herself up with a stick, and she waggled her head when she walked, tok-tok.

One day she set out to visit
her granddaughter.
She left her house, walked
through the markets,
past the river and into the
deep, dark forest.

She had gone only a little way into the forest when a jackal suddenly jumped out from behind a tree. "Ury bop! An old woman!" it cried. "Old woman, I'm going to eat you up!"

“Wait!” she said. “Eat me now, and what will you get but skin and bones? I’m on my way to my granddaughter’s house, and there I’ll grow round and fat.”

“Ach-cha,” said the jackal. “Go and get fat, and when you come back, I’ll eat you.”

The old woman went on her way, leaning on her stick and wagging her head, tok-tok.

A little further on, a tiger jumped out
from behind a tree.
"Ury bop! An old woman!" it said.
"Old woman, I'm going to eat you up."

"Wait!" she cried. "Eat me now, and what will you get but skin and bones? I'm on my way to my granddaughter's house, and there I'll grow round and fat."

"Ach-cha," said the tiger. "Go and get fat, and when you come back, I'll eat you."

So the old woman went on her way, leaning on her stick and wagging her head, tok-tok.

She had almost reached her granddaughter's
house, when suddenly out jumped a bear.
"Ury bop! An old woman!" it said.
"Old woman, I'm going to eat you up!"

"Wait," she said. "Eat me now, and what will you get but skin and bones? I'm on my way to my granddaughter's house, and there I'll grow round and fat."

"Ach-cha," said the bear. "Go and get fat, and when you come back, I'll eat you."

When the old woman got to her
granddaughter's house, she ate curds and curry
and curry and curds and curds and curry and more.
And how fat she got! A little fatter and
she would have burst.

"Dear granddaughter, I must go back home now," she said. "But I'm so fat I can't walk any more. I'll have to go in a cart. A bear and a tiger and a jackal are waiting on the road to eat me up. Ah, me! I don't know what to do!"

“Don’t worry, Deedeema,” said her granddaughter.
“I’ll put you inside this red pumpkin shell,
and the bear and the tiger and the jackal
won’t know you’re there.”

She put the old woman into the pumpkin shell,
along with some tamarinds, plums and rice,
so she would have something to eat.

“Hey-yo!” She gave the pumpkin a push
and it started rolling down
the road.

The pumpkin rolled and the pumpkin rolled, and the old woman inside began to sing,

"Pumpkin, pumpkin,
roll along.
I eat tamarinds, I do.
I eat plums and rice, I do,
While I sing my song."

Now who was waiting in the middle of the road but the bear, who drooled as he thought of the fat old woman he was going to eat. The bear saw the red pumpkin come rolling down the road and heard a voice from inside singing. But the bear only snorted and gave the pumpkin a push with his paw, and it went rolling on down the road.

"What a strange singing pumpkin,"
the bear said to himself as he
watched it roll away. He turned
and followed after it, and inside
the old woman sang,

"Pumpkin, pumpkin, roll along.
I eat tamarinds, I do.
I eat plums and rice, I do,
While I sing my song."

A little further on, the tiger was waiting in the middle of the road, drooling as he thought of the fat old woman he was going to eat. The tiger saw the red pumpkin come rolling along and heard a voice from inside singing. The tiger growled and gave it a push with his paw, and the pumpkin rolled on down the road, with the bear trotting behind it.

"But what a strange singing red pumpkin with a bear behind it," the tiger said to himself, and he trotted along with the bear, while from inside the old woman sang,

"Pumpkin, pumpkin, roll along.
I eat tamarinds, I do.
I eat plums and rice, I do,
While I sing my song."

Still further on, the jackal was waiting in the middle of the road. When the jackal saw the pumpkin come rolling along and heard the voice from inside singing, he jumped up.
"Ho! What's a pumpkin doing singing?" he cried. The jackal hit the red pumpkin with a stick and broke it open, and out popped the old woman.

“Old woman, I’ll eat you up,” said the jackal.
The bear came running up. “Old woman,
I’ll eat you up,” he said.
The tiger came running too. “Old woman,
I’ll eat you up,” he said.
“Of course you will,” the old woman replied,
“and the strongest of you should have my head.”

"I'm strongest!"
cried the bear.

"I'm strongest!"
cried the tiger,
and he grabbed
the bear by the neck.

"I'm strongest!"
cried the jackal,
and he bit the
tiger's tail.

The bear growled,
the tiger roared and
the jackal howled.
What a snarling and
biting and pulling
there was!

And while they were
fighting, the fat old woman
crept away ...